¡A bailar!
Let's Dance!

By / Por Judith Ortiz Cofer

Illustrations by / Ilustraciones de Christina Ann Rodriguez

PIÑATA BOOKS

Piñata Books
Arte Público Press
Houston, Texas

Publication of ¡A bailar! Let's dance! is funded by grants from the City of Houston through the Houston Arts Alliance. We are grateful for their support.

Esta edición de ¡A bailar! Let's dance! ha sido subvencionada por la Ciudad de Houston por medio del Houston Arts Alliance. Les agradecemos su apoyo.

Piñata Books are full of surprises!
¡Piñata Books están llenos de sorpresas!

Piñata Books
An Imprint of Arte Público Press
University of Houston
452 Cullen Performance Hall
Houston, Texas 77204-2004

Cover design by / Diseño de la portada por Mora Des!gn

Cofer, Judith Ortiz, 1952-
    ¡A bailar! Let's Dance! / by Judith Ortiz Cofer ; illustrations by Christina Ann Rodriguez.
        p.   cm.
    Summary: A young girl and her mother put on their red dresses and dance their way through the barrio, collecting friends and neighbors along the way as they go to the park to hear her father's salsa band play.
    ISBN 978-1-55885-698-1 (alk. paper)
    [1. Dance—Fiction. 2. Salsa (Music)—Fiction. 3. Hispanic Americans—Fiction. 4. Bands (Music)—Fiction.] I. Rodriguez, Christina, 1981- ill. II. Title.
    PZ7.O765Bai 2011
    [E]—dc22
                                                                                            2010054522
                                                                                            CIP

Printed in China in May 2011–July 2011 by Creative Printing USA Inc.
12 11 10 9 8 7 6 5 4 3 2 1

This book is for my grandson, Elias John, and with love and gratitude to his parents, Tanya and Dory, who read to Eli every day.

As always, I want to thank John Cofer for his constant encouragement of my work.

Mil gracias to my *compañeras* Billie Bennett Franchini and Kathryn Locey, who offered their comments and expertise as this book evolved over time, until it came to fruition.

— JOC

To my parents Phil and Monica, who paid for all the art lessons and believed in me.

To my sisters Michelle, Jennifer and Brittany, who were asked to stand in as models countless times.

To Jodi and Anna for posing for almost every picture in this book.

And to my mentors Dennis, Doug and Bill, who have made it all possible.

— CAR

It's Saturday afternoon, and Mami and I have been doing our chores
and singing a song we made up to Papi's salsa music.
The rhythm of the music makes us move, move, move.
Mami makes the broom her dance partner, showing me how to dance.

Menéate, menéate, menéate
al ritmo que nos hace . . .
que nos hace feliz . . .

Move, move, move
to the rhythm that makes us . . .
that makes us feel happy . . .

"Listen to the *claves*," Mami says, "and the bongos and the cowbells.
Listen to the maracas and the timbales and the *güiro*!
They'll tell you how to move your shoulders, your hips, your feet."
As I'm putting away the spoons and the forks,
I take two spoons and imitate the *claves*' beat: *uno, dos, tres.*
Mami taps out the salsa rhythm on the floor with the broom.

Al ritmo que nos hace . . .
que nos hace bailar.

To the rhythm that makes us . . .
that makes us dance.

We move, move, move in perfect salsa rhythm, faster, faster, faster.

Menéate, menéate, menéate.

Move, move, move.

We dance faster and faster until we fall down on the kitchen floor laughing.

Menéate, menéate, menéate   *Move, move, move*
al ritmo que nos hace . . .   *to the rhythm that makes us . . .*
que nos hace reír.   *that makes us laugh.*

Mami looks at the kitchen clock. It's three. She lifts me up.
Today we are going to dance salsa for real because Papi's band is playing in the park.
Mami calls her best friend Raquel and says, "*¡A bailar!*
There's salsa music in the park today. Let's dance!"

We put on our red dancing dresses for Papi.
Our dresses balloon out like parachutes
when we twirl and turn in front of the mirror.
As we are dressing we sing,

¡A bailar! al ritmo que nos hace . . .   *Let's dance! to the rhythm that makes us . . .*
que nos hace mover, mover, mover.   *that makes us move, move, move.*

"You look like two beautiful flowers," says Don José
as we pass by the bench where he sits alone most of the day.
"Don José, *vamos*," my mother waves to him.

¡A bailar! al ritmo que nos hace . . .   *Let's dance! to the rhythm that makes us . . .*
que nos hace bailar.   *that makes us dance.*

Don José laughs and follows us slowly.

Al ritmo que nos hace . . .   *To the rhythm that makes us . . .*

His cane is tapping out a salsa beat on the sidewalk.

que nos hace bailar.   *that makes us dance.*

The music from the park floats in and out of our barrio's alleys.
The people in the doorways stop talking to listen.

Menéate, menéate, menéate   *Move, move, move*
al ritmo que nos hace . . .   *to the rhythm that makes us . . .*
bailar, bailar, bailar.   *dance, dance, dance.*

"*¿Adónde van? Where are you going?*" asks a lady in the beauty shop.
She's wearing giant pink rollers and a black cape.
"*¡A bailar!*" Mami yells back, waving for her to join us.
The woman takes Don José's arm. "*¡A bailar, muchachas!*" she calls out.
"*Menéate, menéate, menéate,*" she says to a woman under a hair dryer.
"*Move, move, move,*" she says to the girl looking at the stacks of bottles of shampoo
and lipsticks in every shade of red, and rows and rows of combs and brushes.

¡A bailar! al ritmo que nos hace . . .   *Let's dance! to the rhythm that makes us . . .*

Laughing and singing, the beauty shop women join our parade.

que nos hace reír y cantar . . .   *that makes us laugh and sing . . .*

Two taxi drivers waiting in front of the Gran Fortuna Hotel
see us moving to this rhythm that makes us *cantar, reír, bailar.*
"¡A bailar!" I call out to them.
They turn off the On Duty signs on top of their yellow cars and dance into our line.
The salsa music grows louder as we walk up the block.
"Listen to the *claves*," Mami sings,
"and the bongos, the cowbell, the maracas, the timbales and the *güiro*.
They'll tell you how to move your shoulders, your hips, your feet."

Menéate, menéate, menéate.   *Move, move, move.*

As we go by Mrs. Kim and Mrs. Martínez's fruit stand,
Mami waves and sings, "*¡A bailar!*"
Mrs. Kim smiles and shakes her head "no."
"There are oranges and apples to count,
melons and mangoes to put in brown bags.
And grapes and watermelons to stack in high piles."
Mrs. Kim and Mrs. Martínez bow to each other and do a little dance for us.
Mami and I wave, "*¡Adiós!* See you later!"

¡A bailar! al ritmo que nos hace feliz,
al ritmo que nos hace dos lindas flores
en nuestros vestidos de baile rojos.

Let's dance! to the rhythm that makes us happy,
to the rhythm that makes us two pretty flowers
in our red dancing dresses.

Mami's best friend Raquel and her daughter Risa
are waiting in front of the sign of the big pink pig.
Mami calls out to them, "*¡A bailar!* Let's dance!"
Mami hugs her friend. "¡Hola, Risa! ¡Hola, Raquel!"
Then the four of us hug together making a dancing flower bouquet.

¡A bailar! al ritmo que nos hace . . .   *Let's dance! to the rhythm that makes us . . .*
que nos hace feliz.   *that makes us happy.*

"¡Hola, amigos!" calls out Don Ramón from his bodega.
Mami says his store is filled with smells of her island.
He's moving to the sounds of the salsa.
The music from the plaza is now very loud.
I can hear Papi's trombone calling us to dance.
"Say hello to your papi," Don Ramón says to me. "I'll listen to the music from here.
Menéate, menéate, menéate," he sings and waves to all his customers in our little parade.

We are near the park. I can hear the *claves* marking time
and the *güiro*'s raspy voice saying,
chaski-chis, chaski-chis-chas.
But we cannot cross the street:
Horns are blowing, sirens are screaming and angry people are shouting at each other.
Everyone stops dancing and singing.
There's a policeman in the middle of the street making cars go and stop, and stop and go.
He blows his whistle one, two, three, a million times.
He waves his arms.
"Stop!" he shouts to the truck.
"Stop!" he shouts to the man on his motorcycle.
"Stop!" he shouts to the left.
"Stop!" he shouts to the right.
He waves his hands and then gives one last loud whistle.

Menéate, menéate, menéate.   *Move, move, move.*

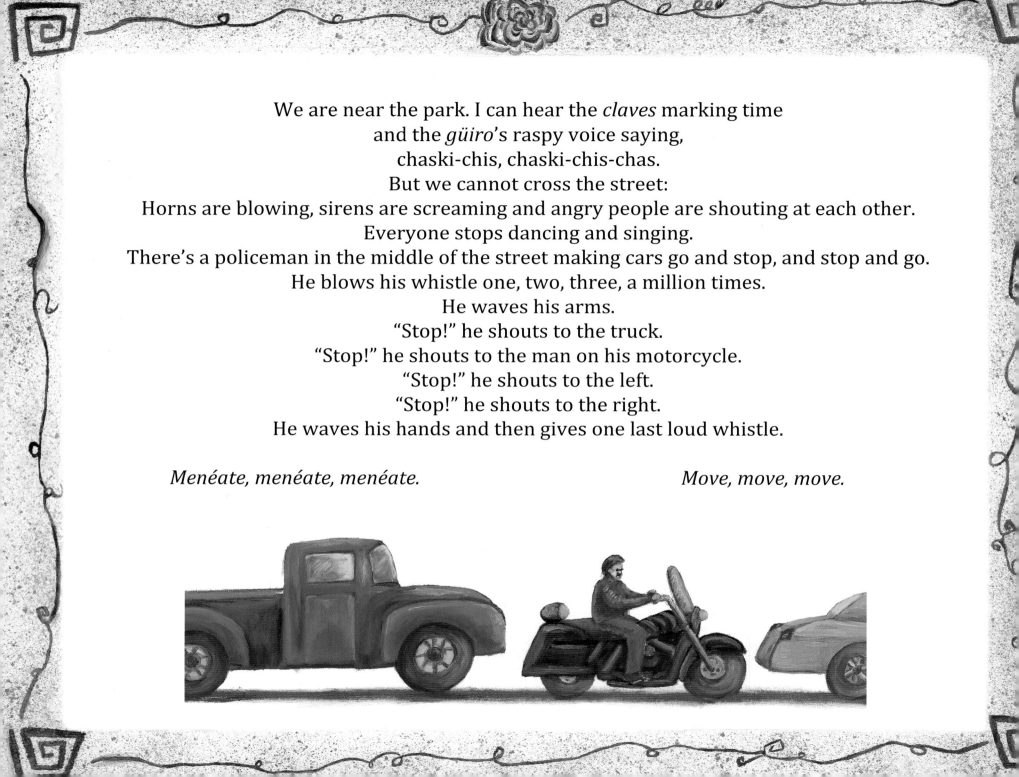

I follow Risa, Mami follows me and we all follow Raquel, dancing, dancing

Al ritmo que nos hace . . .   *To this rhythm . . .*

across the street. *"Gracias, gracias,"* each one of us sings out to the policeman,

que nos hace cantar.   *that makes us sing.*

who's trying out his own dancing steps: "Stop to the right! Stop to the left!"

Que nos hace bailar.   *That makes us dance.*

He's got the rhythm: wave, whistle and start again.
"¡A bailar! Let's dance!" he sings back.

Menéate, menéate, menéate.   *Move, move, move.*

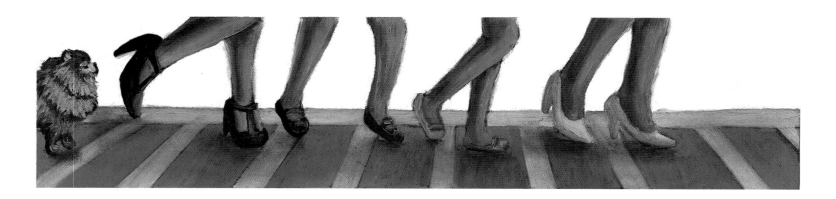

Everyone we meet wants to dance.
The mother with her little baby wants to dance.

Al ritmo que nos hace . . .   *To the rhythm that makes us . . .*

The baby smiles when my mother sings to him,
"¡A bailar, mi hijito, a bailar!"

que nos hace feliz.   *that makes us happy.*

Doña Serena, who sells flowers from her blue truck, wants to dance.

Al ritmo que nos hace . . .   *To the rhythm that makes us . . .*

She gives us red roses to wear in our hair.

que nos hace lindas flores.   *that makes us pretty flowers.*

"Son un jardín de rosas," she says, "a beautiful rose garden."
"Gracias, Doña Serena," I say and twirl and pirouette

Que nos hace bailar.   *That makes us dance.*

so she can see my dress blossom into a red rose.

The boy whooshing by on his skateboard asks, "*¿Adónde van?* Where are you going?"
He's gone before we can answer, "To the park. *¡A bailar!*"
He's back before I can blink my eyes three times.
"*¿A bailar?*" he asks spinning around us.
"To dance?" He's in front.
"*¿A bailar?*" He's in back.
He's swooshing around us, between us, flying by on his skateboard.
He follows the music, and then he's gone
faster than you can say . . . *¡A bailar!* Let's dance!

Even Mr. Reubens, the *artista* who watches and draws birds
and who can sit very still for many hours on the big rock
at the entrance to the park, is tapping his foot to the rhythm.

Al ritmo que nos hace . . .   *To the rhythm that makes us . . .*

"*¡A bailar!* Let's dance," I wave to him.
He puts down his binoculars and laughs when he sees our dancing line.

que nos hace reír.   *that makes us laugh.*

Mr. Reubens waves back. Then he jumps down from the rock to join us.

Que nos hace bailar.   *That makes us dance.*

"Okay, since we cannot fly," he says, "*¡A bailar!* Let's dance!"

In the park, the music is loud,
the bongo drums' ka-thumps, ka-thumps make my heart beat fast.
Mami squeezes my hand to the beat. She leads our parade

Menéate, menéate, menéate.   *Move, move, move.*

into the big crowd that moves together to the rhythm
and sweeps us in like a wave.

Menéate, menéate, menéate.   *Move, move, move.*

I feel like a little fish in a strong current.
I hop up and down,
in and out of the dancing sea,
but I cannot see the stage yet.

Menéate, menéate, menéate   *Move, move, move*

Mami leads me through the waves of arms and legs.
I can hear the scraping song of the *güiro:* chaski-chis, chaski-chis, chas,
and the snaky hiss, hiss, hiss and rattle, rattle, rattle, rattle of the maracas.
And, best of all, the trombone's low Papi-voice calling me . . .

al ritmo que nos hace feliz.   *to the rhythm that makes us happy.*

Raquel and Mami make a chair with their arms and lift me up, up, up.
I see Papi playing his trombone.
I see the bright red shirt I asked him to wear.
Papi steps in front of the band and waves his trombone high in the air.
He plays a few notes that are a secret between him and me,
Te veo, te ve-o, te ve-o.
The trombone's sea-deep voice says to me,
"I see you, Marita, I see you, I see you."
Mami and I squeeze through the swaying shoulders and hips of the barrio.
Almost everyone is here to hear Papi's salsa band play in the park.
When we reach the front of the crowd, Papi goes to the microphone
and his trombone's deep-as-the-sea voice commands,
"¡A bailar, amigos! Let's dance, friends!"
And we all move together.

¡A bailar!
al ritmo que nos hace mover, cantar y reír,
al ritmo que nos hace feliz.
Menéate, menéate, menéate.
Ven conmigo, ¡a bailar!

Let's dance!
to the rhythm that makes us move, sing and dance,
to the rhythm that makes us happy.
Move, move, move.
Come with me, let's dance!

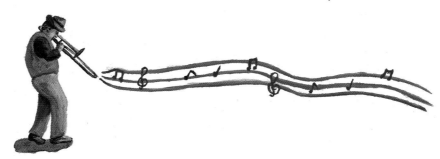

Judith Ortiz Cofer, the Regents' and Franklin Professor of English and Creative Writing at the University of Georgia, is an award-winning poet, novelist and prose writer whose work deals with her bilingual, bicultural experience as a Puerto Rican woman living on the Mainland. She is the author of numerous books, including *Silent Dancing: A Partial Remembrance of a Puerto Rican Childhood*, included in The New York Public Library's *Best Book For The Teen Age 1991* and recipient of a PEN citation, Martha Albrand Award for non-fiction and a Pushcart Prize; and *An Island Like You*, recipient of the Pura Belpré Award and named an ALA Best Book for Young Adults, a *School Library Journal* Best Book of the Year and an ALA Quick Picks for Reluctant Young Adult Readers. Other books for young adults include *The Year of Our Revolution, Call Me María* and *The Meaning of Consuelo*.

Judith Ortiz Cofer, Regents y Franklin Professor de inglés y escritura creativa en la Universidad de Georgia, es una poeta, novelista y narradora reconocida cuyas obras tratan de su experiencia bilingüe y bicultural como una puertorriqueña que vive en Estados Unidos. Es autora de varios libros, entre ellos *Silent Dancing: A Partial Remembrance of a Puerto Rican Childhood,* incluido en la lista *Best Book For The Teen Aged 1991* de la Biblioteca Pública de Nueva York, citado en PEN y merecedor de los premios Martha Albrand para obras no-ficción y Pushcart; y *An Island Like You*, que recibió el premio Pura Belpré y fue nombrado en las listas ALA Best Book for Young Adults, *School Library Journal* Best Book of the Year y ALA Quick Picks for Reluctant Young Adult Readers. Otros de sus libros para jóvenes incluyen *The Year of Our Revolution, Call Me María* y *The Meaning of Consuelo*.

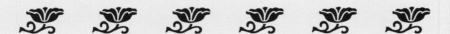

Christina Ann Rodriguez's art career began as a student at the University of Hartford, where she earned her BFA degree in Illustration. She now resides in New Jersey where she helped create *¡A Bailar! Let's Dance!*, her first picture book. Her oil paintings can be seen in other published children's works including *Spider Magazine*. You can view more of her illustrations at www.crodillustration.com.

La carrera de **Christina Ann Rodriguez** empezó como estudiante en la Universidad de Hartford donde se recibió con un título en ilustración. Ahora vive en New Jersey donde ayudó a crear *¡A bailar! Let's Dance!*, su primer libro infantil. Sus óleos figuran en otras publicaciones infantiles como en *Spider Magazine*. Para ver más ilustraciones de Christina visita www.crodillustration.com.